Praise for Annie Proulx's Short Stories

"Geography, splendid and terrible, is a tutelary deity to the characters in *Close Range*. Their lives are futile uphill struggles conducted as a downhill, out-of-control tearaway. Proulx writes of them in a prose that is violent and impacted and mastered just at the point where, having gone all the way to the edge, it is about to go over."

—Richard Eder, *The New York Times Book Review*

"Annie Proulx is a genuine character—a true original. She has a shrewd understanding of people, a strong feeling for landscape . . . and a wry sense of humor rather like Mark Twain's."

—*Los Angeles Times*

"With her biting, invigorating prose, Annie Proulx evokes the expansive landscape her characters hold dear."

—*O, The Oprah Magazine*

"Ms. Proulx writes with all the brutal beauty of one of her Wyoming snowstorms."

—Michael Knight, *The Wall Street Journal*

"It's the prose, as much as the inventiveness of the stories that shines and shines. Every single sentence surprises and delights and just bowls you over."

—Carolyn See, *The Washington Post Book World*

Annie Proulx

Brokeback Mountain

SCRIBNER

New York   London   Toronto   Sydney

SCRIBNER
1230 Avenue of the Americas
New York, NY 10020

First Scribner trade paperback edition 2005

This story originally appeared in *The New Yorker*

For information about special discounts for bulk purchases,
please contact Simon & Schuster Special Sales:
1-800-456-6798 or business@simonandschuster.com

DESIGNED BY ERICH HOBBING

Text set in Bembo

Manufactured in the United States of America

5   7   9   10   8   6

Library of Congress Cataloging-in-Publication Data
Proulx, Annie.
Brokeback Mountain / Annie Proulx.
p. cm.
I. Title.
PS3566.R697B76 2005
813'.54—dc22   2005049988

ISBN-13: 978-0-7432-7132-5
ISBN-10: 0-7432-7132-7

Brokeback Mountain

ENNIS DEL MAR WAKES BEFORE FIVE, WIND ROCKING the trailer, hissing in around the aluminum door and window frames. The shirts hanging on a nail shudder slightly in the draft. He gets up, scratching the grey wedge of belly and pubic hair, shuffles to the gas burner, pours leftover coffee in a chipped enamel pan; the flame swathes it in blue. He turns on the tap and urinates in the sink, pulls on his shirt and jeans, his worn boots, stamping the heels against the floor to get them full on. The wind booms down the curved length of the trailer and under its roaring passage he can hear the scratching of fine gravel and sand. It could be bad on the highway with the horse trailer. He has to be packed and away from the place that morning. Again the ranch is on the market and they've shipped out the last of the horses, paid everybody off the day before, the owner saying, "Give em to the real estate shark, I'm out a here," dropping the keys in Ennis's hand. He might

3

have to stay with his married daughter until he picks up another job, yet he is suffused with a sense of pleasure because Jack Twist was in his dream.

The stale coffee is boiling up but he catches it before it goes over the side, pours it into a stained cup and blows on the black liquid, lets a panel of the dream slide forward. If he does not force his attention on it, it might stoke the day, rewarm that old, cold time on the mountain when they owned the world and nothing seemed wrong. The wind strikes the trailer like a load of dirt coming off a dump truck, eases, dies, leaves a temporary silence.

They were raised on small, poor ranches in opposite corners of the state, Jack Twist in Lightning Flat up on the Montana border, Ennis del Mar from around Sage, near the Utah line, both high school dropout country boys with no prospects, brought up to hard work and privation, both rough-mannered, rough-spoken, inured to the stoic life. Ennis, reared by his older brother and sister after their parents drove off the only curve on Dead Horse Road leaving them twenty-four dollars in cash and a two-mortgage

4

ranch, applied at age fourteen for a hardship license that let him make the hour-long trip from the ranch to the high school. The pickup was old, no heater, one windshield wiper and bad tires; when the transmission went there was no money to fix it. He had wanted to be a sophomore, felt the word carried a kind of distinction, but the truck broke down short of it, pitching him directly into ranch work.

In 1963 when he met Jack Twist, Ennis was engaged to Alma Beers. Both Jack and Ennis claimed to be saving money for a small spread; in Ennis's case that meant a tobacco can with two five-dollar bills inside. That spring, hungry for any job, each had signed up with Farm and Ranch Employment—they came together on paper as herder and camp tender for the same sheep operation north of Signal. The summer range lay above the tree line on Forest Service land on Brokeback Mountain. It would be Jack Twist's second summer on the mountain, Ennis's first. Neither of them was twenty.

They shook hands in the choky little trailer office in front of a table littered with scribbled papers, a Bakelite ashtray brimming with stubs. The venetian blinds hung askew and admitted a triangle of white light, the shadow of the foreman's hand moving into it. Joe Aguirre, wavy hair the color of cigarette ash and parted down the middle, gave them his point of view.

"Forest Service got designated campsites on the allotments. Them camps can be a couple a miles from where we pasture the sheep. Bad predator loss, nobody near lookin after em at night. What I want, camp tender in the main camp where the Forest Service says, but the HERDER"—pointing at Jack with a chop of his hand—"pitch a pup tent on the q.t. with the sheep, out a sight, and he's goin a SLEEP there. Eat supper, breakfast in camp, but SLEEP WITH THE SHEEP, hunderd percent, NO FIRE, don't leave NO SIGN. Roll up that tent every mornin case Forest Service snoops around. Got the dogs, your .30-30, sleep there. Last summer had goddamn near twenty-five percent loss. I don't want that again. YOU," he said to Ennis, taking in the ragged hair, the big nicked hands, the jeans torn, button-gaping shirt, "Fridays twelve noon be down at the bridge with your next week list and mules. Somebody with supplies'll be there in a pickup." He didn't ask if Ennis had a watch but took a cheap round ticker on a braided cord from a box on a high shelf, wound and set it, tossed it to him as if he weren't worth the reach. "TOMORROW MORNIN we'll truck you up the jump-off." Pair of deuces going nowhere.

They found a bar and drank beer through the afternoon, Jack telling Ennis about a lightning storm on the mountain the year before that killed forty-two sheep, the peculiar stink of them and the way they bloated, the need for plenty of whiskey up there. He had shot an eagle, he said, turned his head to show the tail feather in his hatband. At first glance Jack seemed fair enough with his curly hair and quick laugh, but for a small man he carried some weight in the haunch and his smile disclosed buckteeth, not pronounced enough to let him eat popcorn out of the neck of a jug, but noticeable. He was infatuated with the rodeo life and fastened his belt with a minor bull-riding buckle, but his boots were worn to the quick, holed beyond repair and he was crazy to be somewhere, anywhere else than Lightning Flat.

Ennis, high-arched nose and narrow face, was

scruffy and a little cave-chested, balanced a small torso on long, caliper legs, possessed a muscular and supple body made for the horse and for fighting. His reflexes were uncommonly quick and he was farsighted enough to dislike reading anything except Hamley's saddle catalog.

The sheep trucks and horse trailers unloaded at the trailhead and a bandy-legged Basque showed Ennis how to pack the mules, two packs and a riding load on each animal ring-lashed with double diamonds and secured with half hitches, telling him, "Don't never order soup. Them boxes a soup are real bad to pack." Three puppies belonging to one of the blue heelers went in a pack basket, the runt inside Jack's coat, for he loved a little dog. Ennis picked out a big chestnut called Cigar Butt to ride, Jack a bay mare who turned out to have a low startle point. The string of spare horses included a mouse-colored grullo whose looks Ennis liked. Ennis and Jack, the dogs, horses and mules, a thousand ewes and their lambs flowed up the trail like dirty water through the timber and out above the tree line into the great flowery meadows and the coursing, endless wind.

Brokeback Mountain

They got the big tent up on the Forest Service's platform, the kitchen and grub boxes secured. Both slept in camp that first night, Jack already bitching about Joe Aguirre's sleep-with-the-sheep-and-no-fire order, though he saddled the bay mare in the dark morning without saying much. Dawn came glassy orange, stained from below by a gelatinous band of pale green. The sooty bulk of the mountain paled slowly until it was the same color as the smoke from Ennis's breakfast fire. The cold air sweetened, banded pebbles and crumbs of soil cast sudden pencil-long shadows and the rearing lodgepole pines below them massed in slabs of somber malachite.

During the day Ennis looked across a great gulf and sometimes saw Jack, a small dot moving across a high meadow as an insect moves across a tablecloth; Jack, in his dark camp, saw Ennis as night fire, a red spark on the huge black mass of mountain.

Jack came lagging in late one afternoon, drank his two bottles of beer cooled in a wet sack on the shady side of the tent, ate two bowls of stew, four of Ennis's stone biscuits, a can of peaches, rolled a smoke, watched the sun drop.

"I'm commutin four hours a day," he said morosely. "Come in for breakfast, go back to the sheep, evenin get em bedded down, come in for supper, go back to the sheep, spend half the night jumpin up and checkin for coyotes. By rights I should be spendin the night here. Aguirre got no right a make me do this."

"You want a switch?" said Ennis. "I wouldn't mind herdin. I wouldn't mind sleepin out there."

"That ain't the point. Point is, we both should be in this camp. And that goddamn pup tent smells like cat piss or worse."

"Wouldn't mind bein out there."

"Tell you what, you got a get up a dozen times in the night out there over them coyotes. Happy to switch but give you warnin I can't cook worth a shit. Pretty good with a can opener."

"Can't be no worse than me, then. Sure, I wouldn't mind a do it."

They fended off the night for an hour with the yellow kerosene lamp and around ten Ennis rode Cigar

Butt, a good night horse, through the glimmering frost back to the sheep, carrying leftover biscuits, a jar of jam and a jar of coffee with him for the next day saying he'd save a trip, stay out until supper.

"Shot a coyote just first light," he told Jack the next evening, sloshing his face with hot water, lathering up soap and hoping his razor had some cut left in it, while Jack peeled potatoes. "Big son of a bitch. Balls on him size a apples. I bet he'd took a few lambs. Looked like he could a eat a camel. You want some a this hot water? There's plenty."

"It's all yours."

"Well, I'm goin a warsh everthing I can reach," he said, pulling off his boots and jeans (no drawers, no socks, Jack noticed), slopping the green washcloth around until the fire spat.

They had a high-time supper by the fire, a can of beans each, fried potatoes and a quart of whiskey on shares, sat with their backs against a log, boot soles and copper jeans rivets hot, swapping the bottle while the lavender sky emptied of color and the chill air drained down, drinking, smoking cigarettes, getting up every now and then to piss, firelight throwing a

11

sparkle in the arched stream, tossing sticks on the fire to keep the talk going, talking horses and rodeo, roughstock events, wrecks and injuries sustained, the submarine *Thresher* lost two months earlier with all hands and how it must have been in the last doomed minutes, dogs each had owned and known, the draft, Jack's home ranch where his father and mother held on, Ennis's family place folded years ago after his folks died, the older brother in Signal and a married sister in Casper. Jack said his father had been a pretty well known bullrider years back but kept his secrets to himself, never gave Jack a word of advice, never came once to see Jack ride, though he had put him on the woolies when he was a little kid. Ennis said the kind of riding that interested him lasted longer than eight seconds and had some point to it. Money's a good point, said Jack, and Ennis had to agree. They were respectful of each other's opinions, each glad to have a companion where none had been expected. Ennis, riding against the wind back to the sheep in the treacherous, drunken light, thought he'd never had such a good time, felt he could paw the white out of the moon.

Brokeback Mountain

The summer went on and they moved the herd to
new pasture, shifted the camp; the distance between
the sheep and the new camp was greater and the
night ride longer. Ennis rode easy, sleeping with his
eyes open, but the hours he was away from the sheep
stretched out and out. Jack pulled a squalling burr out
of the harmonica, flattened a little from a fall off the
skittish bay mare, and Ennis had a good raspy voice;
a few nights they mangled their way through some
songs. Ennis knew the salty words to "Strawberry
Roan." Jack tried a Carl Perkins song, bawling "what
I say-ay-ay," but he favored a sad hymn, "Water-
Walking Jesus," learned from his mother who
believed in the Pentecost, that he sang at dirge slow-
ness, setting off distant coyote yips.

"Too late to go out to them damn sheep," said
Ennis, dizzy drunk on all fours one cold hour when
the moon had notched past two. The meadow stones
glowed white-green and a flinty wind worked over
the meadow, scraped the fire low, then ruffled it into
yellow silk sashes. "Got you a extra blanket I'll roll
up out here and grab forty winks, ride out at first
light."

"Freeze your ass off when that fire dies down. Better off sleepin in the tent."

"Doubt I'll feel nothin." But he staggered under canvas, pulled his boots off, snored on the ground cloth for a while, woke Jack with the clacking of his jaw.

"Jesus Christ, quit hammerin and get over here. Bedroll's big enough," said Jack in an irritable sleep-clogged voice. It was big enough, warm enough, and in a little while they deepened their intimacy considerably. Ennis ran full-throttle on all roads whether fence mending or money spending, and he wanted none of it when Jack seized his left hand and brought it to his erect cock. Ennis jerked his hand away as though he'd touched fire, got to his knees, unbuckled his belt, shoved his pants down, hauled Jack onto all fours and, with the help of the clear slick and a little spit, entered him, nothing he'd done before but no instruction manual needed. They went at it in silence except for a few sharp intakes of breath and Jack's choked "gun's goin *off*," then out, down, and asleep.

Ennis woke in red dawn with his pants around his knees, a top-grade headache, and Jack butted against him; without saying anything about it both knew how it would go for the rest of the summer, sheep be damned.

As it did go. They never talked about the sex, let it happen, at first only in the tent at night, then in the full daylight with the hot sun striking down, and at evening in the fire glow, quick, rough, laughing and snorting, no lack of noises, but saying not a goddamn word except once Ennis said, "I'm not no queer," and Jack jumped in with "Me neither. A one-shot thing. Nobody's business but ours." There were only the two of them on the mountain flying in the euphoric, bitter air, looking down on the hawk's back and the crawling lights of vehicles on the plain below, suspended above ordinary affairs and distant from tame ranch dogs barking in the dark hours. They believed themselves invisible, not knowing Joe Aguirre had watched them through his 10x42 binoculars for ten minutes one day, waiting until they'd buttoned up their jeans, waiting until Ennis rode back to the sheep, before bringing up the message that Jack's people had sent word that his uncle Harold was in the hospital with pneumonia and expected not to make it. Though he did, and Aguirre came up again to say so, fixing Jack with his bold stare, not bothering to dismount.

In August Ennis spent the whole night with Jack in the main camp and in a blowy hailstorm the sheep took off west and got among a herd in another allotment. There was a damn miserable time for five days, Ennis and a Chilean herder with no English trying to sort them out, the task almost impossible as the paint brands were worn and faint at this late season. Even when the numbers were right Ennis knew the sheep were mixed. In a disquieting way everything seemed mixed.

The first snow came early, on August thirteenth, piling up a foot, but was followed by a quick melt. The next week Joe Aguirre sent word to bring them down—another, bigger storm was moving in from the Pacific—and they packed in the game and moved off the mountain with the sheep, stones rolling at their heels, purple cloud crowding in from the west and the metal smell of coming snow pressing them on. The mountain boiled with demonic energy, glazed with flickering broken-cloud light, the wind combed the grass and drew from the damaged krummholz and slit rock a bestial drone. As they descended the slope Ennis felt he was in a slow-motion, but headlong, irreversible fall.

Joe Aguirre paid them, said little. He had looked at the milling sheep with a sour expression, said, "Some a these never went up there with you." The count was not what he'd hoped for either. Ranch stiffs never did much of a job.

"You goin a do this next summer?" said Jack to Ennis in the street, one leg already up in his green pickup. The wind was gusting hard and cold.

"Maybe not." A dust plume rose and hazed the air with fine grit and he squinted against it. "Like I said, Alma and me's gettin married in December. Try to get somethin on a ranch. You?" He looked away from Jack's jaw, bruised blue from the hard punch Ennis had thrown him on the last day.

"If nothin better comes along. Thought some about going back up to my daddy's place, give him a hand over the winter, then maybe head out for Texas in the spring. If the draft don't get me."

"Well, see you around, I guess." The wind tumbled an empty feed bag down the street until it fetched up under his truck.

"Right," said Jack, and they shook hands, hit each other on the shoulder, then there was forty feet of distance between them and nothing to do but drive away in opposite directions. Within a mile Ennis felt like someone was pulling his guts out hand over hand a yard at a time. He stopped at the side of the road and, in the whirling new snow, tried to puke but nothing came up. He felt about as bad as he ever had and it took a long time for the feeling to wear off.

In December Ennis married Alma Beers and had her pregnant by mid-January. He picked up a few short-lived ranch jobs, then settled in as a wrangler on the old Elwood Hi-Top place north of Lost Cabin in Washakie County. He was still working there in September when Alma Jr., as he called his daughter, was born and their bedroom was full of the smell of old blood and milk and baby shit, and the sounds were of squalling and sucking and Alma's sleepy groans, all reassuring of fecundity and life's continuance to one who worked with livestock.

When the Hi-Top folded they moved to a small apartment in Riverton up over a laundry. Ennis got on the highway crew, tolerating it but working weekends at the Rafter B in exchange for keeping his horses out there. The second girl was born and Alma wanted to stay in town near the clinic because the child had an asthmatic wheeze.

"Ennis, please, no more damn lonesome ranches for us," she said, sitting on his lap, wrapping her thin, freckled arms around him. "Let's get a place here in town?"

"I guess," said Ennis, slipping his hand up her blouse sleeve and stirring the silky armpit hair, then easing her down, fingers moving up her ribs to the jelly breast, over the round belly and knee and up into the wet gap all the way to the north pole or the equator depending which way you thought you were sailing, working at it until she shuddered and bucked against his hand and he rolled her over, did quickly what she hated. They stayed in the little apartment which he favored because it could be left at any time.

*   *   *

The fourth summer since Brokeback Mountain came on and in June Ennis had a general delivery letter from Jack Twist, the first sign of life in all that time.

Friend this letter is a long time over due. Hope you get it. Heard you was in Riverton. Im coming thru on the 24th, thought Id stop and buy you a beer. Drop me a line if you can, say if your there.

The return address was Childress, Texas. Ennis wrote back, *you bet,* gave the Riverton address.

The day was hot and clear in the morning, but by noon the clouds had pushed up out of the west rolling a little sultry air before them. Ennis, wearing his best shirt, white with wide black stripes, didn't know what time Jack would get there and so had taken the day off, paced back and forth, looking down into a street pale with dust. Alma was saying something about taking his friend to the Knife & Fork for supper instead of cooking it was so hot, if they could get a baby-sitter, but Ennis said more likely he'd just go out with Jack and get drunk. Jack was not a restaurant type, he said, thinking of the dirty spoons sticking out of the cans of cold beans balanced on the log.

Late in the afternoon, thunder growling, that same old green pickup rolled in and he saw Jack get out of the truck, beat-up Resistol tilted back. A hot jolt scalded Ennis and he was out on the landing pulling the door closed behind him. Jack took the stairs two and two. They seized each other by the shoulders, hugged mightily, squeezing the breath out of each other, saying, son of a bitch, son of a bitch, then, and easily as the right key turns the lock tumblers, their mouths came together, and hard, Jack's big teeth bringing blood, his hat falling to the floor, stubble rasping, wet saliva welling, and the door opening and Alma looking out for a few seconds at Ennis's straining shoulders and shutting the door again and still they clinched, pressing chest and groin and thigh and leg together, treading on each other's toes until they pulled apart to breathe and Ennis, not big on endearments, said what he said to his horses and daughters, little darlin.

The door opened again a few inches and Alma stood in the narrow light.

What could he say? "Alma, this is Jack Twist, Jack, my wife Alma." His chest was heaving. He could smell Jack—the intensely familiar odor of cigarettes, musky sweat and a faint sweetness like grass, and with it the rushing cold of the mountain. "Alma," he said, "Jack and me ain't seen each other in four years." As if it were a reason. He was glad the light was dim on the landing but did not turn away from her.

"Sure enough," said Alma in a low voice. She had seen what she had seen. Behind her in the room lightning lit the window like a white sheet waving and the baby cried.

"You got a kid?" said Jack. His shaking hand grazed Ennis's hand, electrical current snapped between them.

"Two little girls," Ennis said. "Alma Jr. and Francine. Love them to pieces." Alma's mouth twitched.

"I got a boy," said Jack. "Eight months old. Tell you what, I married a cute little old Texas girl down in Childress—Lureen." From the vibration of the floorboard on which they both stood Ennis could feel how hard Jack was shaking.

"Alma," he said. "Jack and me is goin out and get a drink. Might not get back tonight, we get drinkin and talkin."

"Sure enough," Alma said, taking a dollar bill from her pocket. Ennis guessed she was going to ask him to get her a pack of cigarettes, bring him back sooner.

"Please to meet you," said Jack, trembling like a run-out horse.

"Ennis—" said Alma in her misery voice, but that didn't slow him down on the stairs and he called back, "Alma, you want smokes there's some in the pocket a my blue shirt in the bedroom."

They went off in Jack's truck, bought a bottle of whiskey and within twenty minutes were in the Motel Siesta jouncing a bed. A few handfuls of hail rattled against the window followed by rain and slippery wind banging the unsecured door of the next room then and through the night.

The room stank of semen and smoke and sweat and whiskey, of old carpet and sour hay, saddle leather, shit and cheap soap. Ennis lay spread-eagled, spent and wet, breathing deep, still half tumescent, Jack blowing forceful cigarette clouds like whale spouts, and Jack said, "Christ, it got a be all that time a yours ahorseback makes it so goddamn good. We got to talk about this. Swear to god I didn't know we was goin a get into this again—yeah, I did. Why I'm here. I fuckin knew it. Redlined all the way, couldn't get here fast enough."

"I didn't know where in the *hell* you was," said Ennis. "Four years. I about give up on you. I figured you was sore about that punch."

"Friend," said Jack, "I was in Texas rodeoin. How I met Lureen. Look over on that chair."

On the back of the soiled orange chair he saw the shine of a buckle. "Bullridin?"

"Yeah. I made three fuckin thousand dollars that year. Fuckin starved. Had to borrow everthing but a toothbrush from other guys. Drove grooves across Texas. Half the time under that cunt truck fixin it. Anyway, I didn't never think about losin. Lureen? There's some serious money there. Her old man's got it. Got this farm machinery business. Course he don't let her have none a the money, and he hates my fuckin guts, so it's a hard go now but one a these days—"

"Well, you're goin a go where you look. Army didn't get you?" The thunder sounded far to the east, moving from them in its red wreaths of light.

"They can't get no use out a me. Got some crushed vertebrates. And a stress fracture, the arm bone here, you know how bullridin you're always leverin it off your thigh?—she gives a little ever time you do it. Even if you tape it good you break it a little goddamn bit at a time. Tell you what, hurts like a bitch afterwards. Had a busted leg. Busted in three places. Come off the bull and it was a big bull with a lot a drop, he got rid a me in about three flat and he come after me and he was sure faster. Lucky enough. Friend a mine got his oil checked with a horn dipstick and that was all she wrote. Bunch a other things, fuckin busted ribs, sprains and pains, torn ligaments. See, it ain't like it was in my daddy's time. It's guys with money go to college, trained athaletes. You got a have some money to rodeo now. Lureen's old man wouldn't give me a dime if I dropped it, except one way. And I know enough about the game now so I see that I ain't never goin a be on the bubble. Other reasons. I'm gettin out while I still can walk."

Ennis pulled Jack's hand to his mouth, took a hit from the cigarette, exhaled. "Sure as hell seem in one piece to me. You know, I was sittin up here all that time tryin to figure out if I was—? I know I ain't. I mean here we both got wives and kids, right? I like doin it with women, yeah, but Jesus H., ain't nothin like this. I never had no thoughts a doin it with another guy except I sure wrang it out a hunderd times thinkin about you. You do it with other guys? Jack?"

"Shit no," said Jack, who had been riding more than bulls, not rolling his own. "You know that. Old Brokeback got us good and it sure ain't over. We got a work out what the fuck we're goin a do now."

"That summer," said Ennis. "When we split up after we got paid out I had gut cramps so bad I pulled over and tried to puke, thought I ate somethin bad at that place in Dubois. Took me about a year a figure out it was that I shouldn't a let you out a my sights. Too late then by a long, long while."

"Friend," said Jack. "We got us a fuckin situation here. Got a figure out what to do."

"I doubt there's nothin now we can do," said Ennis. "What I'm sayin, Jack, I built a life up in them years. Love my little girls. Alma? It ain't her fault. You got your baby and wife, that place in Texas. You and me can't hardly be decent together if what happened back there"—he jerked his head in the direction of the apartment—"grabs on us like that. We do that in the wrong place we'll be dead. There's no reins on this one. It scares the piss out a me."

"Got to tell you, friend, maybe somebody seen us that summer. I was back there the next June, thinkin about goin back—I didn't, lit out for Texas instead— and Joe Aguirre's in the office and he says to me, he says, 'You boys found a way to make the time pass up there, didn't you,' and I give him a look but when I went out I seen he had a big-ass pair a binoculars hangin off his rearview." He neglected to add that the foreman had leaned back in his squeaky wooden tilt chair, said, Twist, you guys wasn't gettin paid to leave the dogs baby-sit the sheep while you stemmed the rose, and declined to rehire him. He went on, "Yeah, that little punch a yours surprised me. I never figured you to throw a dirty punch."

27

"I come up under my brother K.E., three years older'n me, slugged me silly ever day. Dad got tired a me come bawlin in the house and when I was about six he set me down and says, Ennis, you got a problem and you got a fix it or it's gonna be with you until you're ninety and K.E.'s ninety-three. Well, I says, he's bigger'n me. Dad says, you got a take him unawares, don't say nothin to him, make him feel some pain, get out fast and keep doin it until he takes the message. Nothin like hurtin somebody to make him hear good. So I did. I got him in the outhouse, jumped him on the stairs, come over to his pillow in the night while he was sleepin and pasted him damn good. Took about two days. Never had trouble with K.E. since. The lesson was, don't say nothin and get it over with quick." A telephone rang in the next room, rang on and on, stopped abruptly in mid-peal.

"You won't catch me again," said Jack. "Listen. I'm thinkin, tell you what, if you and me had a little ranch together, little cow and calf operation, your horses, it'd be some sweet life. Like I said, I'm gettin out a rodeo. I ain't no broke-dick rider but I don't got the bucks a ride out this slump I'm in and I don't got the bones a keep gettin wrecked. I got it figured, got this plan, Ennis, how we can do it, you and me. Lureen's old man, you bet he'd give me a bunch if I'd get lost. Already more or less said it—"

"Whoa, whoa, whoa. It ain't goin a be that way. We can't. I'm stuck with what I got, caught in my own loop. Can't get out of it. Jack, I don't want a be like them guys you see around sometimes. And I don't want a be dead. There was these two old guys ranched together down home, Earl and Rich—Dad would pass a remark when he seen them. They was a joke even though they was pretty tough old birds. I was what, nine years old and they found Earl dead in a irrigation ditch. They'd took a tire iron to him, spurred him up, drug him around by his dick until it pulled off, just bloody pulp. What the tire iron done looked like pieces a burned tomatoes all over him, nose tore down from skiddin on gravel."

"You seen that?"

"Dad made sure I seen it. Took me to see it. Me and K.E. Dad laughed about it. Hell, for all I know he done the job. If he was alive and was to put his head in that door right now you bet he'd go get his tire

29

iron. Two guys livin together? No. All I can see is we get together once in a while way the hell out in the back a nowhere—"

"How much is once in a while?" said Jack. "Once in a while ever four fuckin years?"

"No," said Ennis, forbearing to ask whose fault that was. "I goddamn hate it that you're goin a drive away in the mornin and I'm goin back to work. But if you can't fix it you got a stand it," he said. "Shit. I been lookin at people on the street. This happen a other people? What the hell do they do?"

"It don't happen in Wyomin and if it does I don't know what they do, maybe go to Denver," said Jack, sitting up, turning away from him, "and I don't give a flyin fuck. Son of a bitch, Ennis, take a couple days off. Right now. Get us out a here. Throw your stuff in the back a my truck and let's get up in the mountains. Couple a days. Call Alma up and tell her you're goin. Come on, Ennis, you just shot my airplane out a the sky—give me somethin a go on. This ain't no little thing that's happenin here."

The hollow ringing began again in the next room,

and as if he were answering it, Ennis picked up the phone on the bedside table, dialed his own number.

A slow corrosion worked between Ennis and Alma, no real trouble, just widening water. She was working at a grocery store clerk job, saw she'd always have to work to keep ahead of the bills on what Ennis made. Alma asked Ennis to use rubbers because she dreaded another pregnancy. He said no to that, said he would be happy to leave her alone if she didn't want any more of his kids. Under her breath she said, "I'd have em if you'd support em." And under that, thought, anyway, what you like to do don't make too many babies.

Her resentment opened out a little every year: the embrace she had glimpsed, Ennis's fishing trips once or twice a year with Jack Twist and never a vacation with her and the girls, his disinclination to step out and have any fun, his yearning for low-paid, long-houred ranch work, his propensity to roll to the wall and sleep as soon as he hit the bed, his failure to look for a decent permanent job with the county or the power company, put her in a long, slow dive and when Alma Jr. was nine and Francine seven she said, what am I doin hangin around with him, divorced Ennis and married the Riverton grocer.

Ennis went back to ranch work, hired on here and there, not getting much ahead but glad enough to be around stock again, free to drop things, quit if he had to, and go into the mountains at short notice. He had no serious hard feelings, just a vague sense of getting shortchanged, and showed it was all right by taking Thanksgiving dinner with Alma and her grocer and the kids, sitting between his girls and talking horses to them, telling jokes, trying not to be a sad daddy. After the pie Alma got him off in the kitchen, scraped the plates and said she worried about him and he ought to get married again. He saw she was pregnant, about four, five months, he guessed.

"Once burned," he said, leaning against the counter, feeling too big for the room.

"You still go fishin with that Jack Twist?"

"Some." He thought she'd take the pattern off the plate with the scraping.

"You know," she said, and from her tone he knew something was coming, "I used to wonder how come you never brought any trouts home. Always said you caught plenty. So one time I got your creel case open the night before you went on one a your little trips—price tag still on it after five years—and I tied a note on the end of the line. It said, hello Ennis, bring some fish home, love, Alma. And then you come back and said you'd caught a bunch a browns and ate them up. Remember? I looked in the case when I got a chance and there was my note still tied there and that line hadn't touched water in its life." As though the word "water" had called out its domestic cousin she twisted the faucet, sluiced the plates.

"That don't mean nothin."

"Don't lie, don't try to fool me, Ennis. I know what it means. Jack Twist? Jack Nasty. You and him—"

She'd overstepped his line. He seized her wrist; tears sprang and rolled, a dish clattered.

"Shut up," he said. "Mind your own business. You don't know nothin about it."

"I'm goin a yell for Bill."

"You fuckin go right ahead. Go on and fuckin yell. I'll make him eat the fuckin floor and you too." He gave another wrench that left her with a burning bracelet, shoved his hat on backwards and slammed out. He went to the Black and Blue Eagle bar that night, got drunk, had a short dirty fight and left. He didn't try to see his girls for a long time, figuring they would look him up when they got the sense and years to move out from Alma.

They were no longer young men with all of it before them. Jack had filled out through the shoulders and hams, Ennis stayed as lean as a clothes-pole, stepped around in worn boots, jeans and shirts summer and winter, added a canvas coat in cold weather. A benign growth appeared on his eyelid and gave it a drooping appearance, a broken nose healed crooked.

Years on years they worked their way through the high meadows and mountain drainages, horse-packing into the Big Horns, Medicine Bows, south end of the Gallatins, Absarokas, Granites, Owl Creeks, the Bridger-Teton Range, the Freezeouts

and the Shirleys, Ferrises and the Rattlesnakes, Salt
River Range, into the Wind Rivers over and again,
the Sierra Madres, Gros Ventres, the Washakies,
Laramies, but never returning to Brokeback.

Down in Texas Jack's father-in-law died and
Lureen, who inherited the farm equipment business, showed a skill for management and hard deals.
Jack found himself with a vague managerial title,
traveling to stock and agricultural machinery shows.
He had some money now and found ways to spend it
on his buying trips. A little Texas accent flavored his
sentences, "cow" twisted into "kyow" and "wife"
coming out as "waf." He'd had his front teeth filed
down and capped, said he'd felt no pain, and to finish
the job grew a heavy mustache.

In May of 1983 they spent a few cold days at a series
of little icebound, no-name high lakes, then worked
across into the Hail Strew River drainage.

Going up, the day was fine but the trail deep-
drifted and slopping wet at the margins. They left it to
wind through a slashy cut, leading the horses through

brittle branchwood, Jack, the same eagle feather in his old hat, lifting his head in the heated noon to take the air scented with resinous lodgepole, the dry needle duff and hot rock, bitter juniper crushed beneath the horses' hooves. Ennis, weather-eyed, looked west for the heated cumulus that might come up on such a day but the boneless blue was so deep, said Jack, that he might drown looking up.

Around three they swung through a narrow pass to a southeast slope where the strong spring sun had had a chance to work, dropped down to the trail again which lay snowless below them. They could hear the river muttering and making a distant train sound a long way off. Twenty minutes on they surprised a black bear on the bank above them rolling a log over for grubs and Jack's horse shied and reared, Jack saying "Wo! Wo!" and Ennis's bay dancing and snorting but holding. Jack reached for the .30-06 but there was no need; the startled bear galloped into the trees with the lumpish gait that made it seem it was falling apart.

The tea-colored river ran fast with snowmelt, a scarf of bubbles at every high rock, pools and setbacks streaming. The ochre-branched willows swayed stiffly, pollened catkins like yellow thumbprints. The horses drank and Jack dismounted, scooped icy water up in his hand, crystalline drops falling from his fingers, his mouth and chin glistening with wet.

"Get beaver fever doin that," said Ennis, then, "Good enough place," looking at the level bench above the river, two or three fire-rings from old hunting camps. A sloping meadow rose behind the bench, protected by a stand of lodgepole. There was plenty of dry wood. They set up camp without saying much, picketed the horses in the meadow. Jack broke the seal on a bottle of whiskey, took a long, hot swallow, exhaled forcefully, said, "That's one a the two things I need right now," capped and tossed it to Ennis.

On the third morning there were the clouds Ennis had expected, a grey racer out of the west, a bar of darkness driving wind before it and small flakes. It faded after an hour into tender spring snow that heaped wet and heavy. By nightfall it turned colder. Jack and Ennis passed a joint back and forth, the fire burning late, Jack restless and bitching about the cold, poking the flames with a stick, twisting the dial of the transistor radio until the batteries died.

Ennis said he'd been putting the blocks to a woman who worked part-time at the Wolf Ears bar in Signal where he was working now for Stoutamire's cow and calf outfit, but it wasn't going anywhere and she had some problems he didn't want. Jack said he'd had a thing going with the wife of a rancher down the road in Childress and for the last few months he'd slank around expecting to get shot by Lureen or the husband, one. Ennis laughed a little and said he probably deserved it. Jack said he was doing all right but he missed Ennis bad enough sometimes to make him whip babies.

The horses nickered in the darkness beyond the fire's circle of light. Ennis put his arm around Jack, pulled him close, said he saw his girls about once a month, Alma Jr. a shy seventeen-year-old with his beanpole length, Francine a little live wire. Jack slid his cold hand between Ennis's legs, said he was worried about his boy who was, no doubt about it, dyslexic or something, couldn't get anything right, fifteen years old and couldn't hardly read, *he* could see it though goddamn Lureen wouldn't admit to it and pretended the kid was o.k., refused to get any bitchin kind a help about it. He didn't know what the fuck the answer was. Lureen had the money and called the shots.

"I used a want a boy for a kid," said Ennis, undoing buttons, "but just got little girls."

"I didn't want none a either kind," said Jack. "But fuck-all has worked the way I wanted. Nothin never come to my hand the right way." Without getting up he threw deadwood on the fire, the sparks flying up with their truths and lies, a few hot points of fire landing on their hands and faces, not for the first time, and they rolled down into the dirt. One thing never changed: the brilliant charge of their infrequent couplings was darkened by the sense of time flying, never enough time, never enough.

A day or two later in the trailhead parking lot, horses loaded into the trailer, Ennis was ready to head back to Signal, Jack up to Lightning Flat to see the old man. Ennis leaned into Jack's window, said what he'd been putting off the whole week, that likely he couldn't get away again until November after they'd shipped stock and before winter feeding started.

"November. What in hell happened a August? Tell you what, we said August, nine, ten days. Christ, Ennis! Whyn't you tell me this before? You had a fuckin week to say some little word about it. And why's it we're always in the friggin cold weather? We ought a do somethin. We ought a go south. We ought a go to Mexico one day."

"Mexico? Jack, you know me. All the travelin I ever done is goin around the coffeepot lookin for the handle. And I'll be runnin the baler all August, that's what's the matter with August. Lighten up, Jack. We can hunt in November, kill a nice elk. Try if I can get Don Wroe's cabin again. We had a good time that year."

"You know, friend, this is a goddamn bitch of a unsatisfactory situation. You used a come away easy. It's like seein the pope now."

"Jack, I got a work. Them earlier days I used a quit the jobs. You got a wife with money, a good job. You forget how it is bein broke all the time. You ever hear a child support? I been payin out for years and got more to go. Let me tell you, I can't quit this one. And I can't get the time off. It was tough gettin this time—some a them late heifers is still calvin. You don't leave then. You don't. Stoutamire is a hell-raiser and he raised hell about me takin the week. I don't blame him. He probly ain't got a night's sleep since I left. The trade-off was August. You got a better idea?"

"I did once." The tone was bitter and accusatory.

Ennis said nothing, straightened up slowly, rubbed at his forehead; a horse stamped inside the trailer. He walked to his truck, put his hand on the trailer, said something that only the horses could hear, turned and walked back at a deliberate pace.

"You been a Mexico, Jack?" Mexico was the place. He'd heard. He was cutting fence now, trespassing in the shoot-em zone.

"Hell yes, I been. Where's the fuckin problem?" Braced for it all these years and here it came, late and unexpected.

"I got a say this to you one time, Jack, and I ain't foolin. What I don't know," said Ennis, "all them things I don't know could get you killed if I should come to know them."

41

"Try this one," said Jack, "and *I'll* say it just one time. Tell you what, we could a had a good life together, a fuckin real good life. You wouldn't do it, Ennis, so what we got now is Brokeback Mountain. Everthing built on that. It's all we got, boy, fuckin all, so I hope you know that if you don't never know the rest. Count the damn few times we been together in twenty years. Measure the fuckin short leash you keep me on, then ask me about Mexico and then tell me you'll kill me for needin it and not hardly never gettin it. You got no fuckin idea how bad it gets. I'm not you. I can't make it on a couple a high-altitude fucks once or twice a year. You're too much for me, Ennis, you son of a whoreson bitch. I wish I knew how to quit you."

Like vast clouds of steam from thermal springs in winter the years of things unsaid and now unsayable—admissions, declarations, shames, guilts, fears—rose around them. Ennis stood as if heart-shot, face grey and deep-lined, grimacing, eyes screwed shut, fists clenched, legs caving, hit the ground on his knees.

"Jesus," said Jack. "Ennis?" But before he was out

of the truck, trying to guess if it was heart attack or the overflow of an incendiary rage, Ennis was back on his feet and somehow, as a coat hanger is straightened to open a locked car and then bent again to its original shape, they torqued things almost to where they had been, for what they'd said was no news. Nothing ended, nothing begun, nothing resolved.

What Jack remembered and craved in a way he could neither help nor understand was the time that distant summer on Brokeback when Ennis had come up behind him and pulled him close, the silent embrace satisfying some shared and sexless hunger.

They had stood that way for a long time in front of the fire, its burning tossing ruddy chunks of light, the shadow of their bodies a single column against the rock. The minutes ticked by from the round watch in Ennis's pocket, from the sticks in the fire settling into coals. Stars bit through the wavy heat layers above the fire. Ennis's breath came slow and quiet, he hummed, rocked a little in the sparklight and Jack leaned against the steady heartbeat, the vibrations of the humming like faint electricity and, standing, he fell into sleep that was not sleep but something else drowsy and tranced until Ennis, dredging up a rusty but still useable phrase from the childhood time before his mother died, said, "Time to hit the hay, cowboy. I got a go. Come on, you're sleepin on your feet like a horse," and gave Jack a shake, a push, and went off in the darkness. Jack heard his spurs tremble as he mounted, the words "see you tomorrow," and the horse's shuddering snort, grind of hoof on stone.

Later, that dozy embrace solidified in his memory as the single moment of artless, charmed happiness in their separate and difficult lives. Nothing marred it, even the knowledge that Ennis would not then embrace him face to face because he did not want to see nor feel that it was Jack he held. And maybe, he thought, they'd never got much farther than that. Let be, let be.

Ennis didn't know about the accident for months until his postcard to Jack saying that November still looked like the first chance came back stamped

DECEASED. He called Jack's number in Childress, something he had done only once before when Alma divorced him and Jack had misunderstood the reason for the call, had driven twelve hundred miles north for nothing. This would be all right, Jack would answer, had to answer. But he did not. It was Lureen and she said who? who is this? and when he told her again she said in a level voice yes, Jack was pumping up a flat on the truck out on a back road when the tire blew up. The bead was damaged somehow and the force of the explosion slammed the rim into his face, broke his nose and jaw and knocked him unconscious on his back. By the time someone came along he had drowned in his own blood.

No, he thought, they got him with the tire iron.

"Jack used to mention you," she said. "You're the fishing buddy or the hunting buddy, I know that. Would have let you know," she said, "but I wasn't sure about your name and address. Jack kept most a his friends' addresses in his head. It was a terrible thing. He was only thirty-nine years old."

The huge sadness of the northern plains rolled down on him. He didn't know which way it was, the

tire iron or a real accident, blood choking down
Jack's throat and nobody to turn him over. Under the
wind drone he heard steel slamming off bone, the
hollow chatter of a settling tire rim.

"He buried down there?" He wanted to curse her
for letting Jack die on the dirt road.

The little Texas voice came slip-sliding down the
wire. "We put a stone up. He use to say he wanted to
be cremated, ashes scattered on Brokeback Mountain.
I didn't know where that was. So he was cremated,
like he wanted, and like I say, half his ashes was
interred here, and the rest I sent up to his folks. I
thought Brokeback Mountain was around where he
grew up. But knowing Jack, it might be some pretend
place where the bluebirds sing and there's a whiskey
spring."

"We herded sheep on Brokeback one summer,"
said Ennis. He could hardly speak.

"Well, he said it was his place. I thought he meant
to get drunk. Drink whiskey up there. He drank a
lot."

"His folks still up in Lightnin Flat?"

"Oh yeah. They'll be there until they die. I never

met them. They didn't come down for the funeral.
You get in touch with them. I suppose they'd appre-
ciate it if his wishes was carried out."

No doubt about it, she was polite but the little
voice was cold as snow.

The road to Lightning Flat went through desolate
country past a dozen abandoned ranches distributed
over the plain at eight- and ten-mile intervals, houses
sitting blank-eyed in the weeds, corral fences down.
The mailbox read John C. Twist. The ranch was a
meagre little place, leafy spurge taking over. The
stock was too far distant for him to see their condi-
tion, only that they were black baldies. A porch
stretched across the front of the tiny brown stucco
house, four rooms, two down, two up.

Ennis sat at the kitchen table with Jack's father.
Jack's mother, stout and careful in her movements as
though recovering from an operation, said, "Want
some coffee, don't you? Piece a cherry cake?"

"Thank you, ma'am, I'll take a cup a coffee but I
can't eat no cake just now."

The old man sat silent, his hands folded on the plastic tablecloth, staring at Ennis with an angry, knowing expression. Ennis recognized in him a not uncommon type with the hard need to be the stud duck in the pond. He couldn't see much of Jack in either one of them, took a breath.

"I feel awful bad about Jack. Can't begin to say how bad I feel. I knew him a long time. I come by to tell you that if you want me to take his ashes up there on Brokeback like his wife says he wanted I'd be proud to."

There was a silence. Ennis cleared his throat but said nothing more.

The old man said, "Tell you what, I know where Brokeback Mountain is. He thought he was too goddamn special to be buried in the family plot."

Jack's mother ignored this, said, "He used a come home every year, even after he was married and down in Texas, and help his daddy on the ranch for a week, fix the gates and mow and all. I kept his room like it was when he was a boy and I think he appreciated that. You are welcome to go up in his room if you want."

48

The old man spoke angrily. "I can't get no help out here. Jack used a say, 'Ennis del Mar,' he used a say, 'I'm goin a bring him up here one a these days and we'll lick this damn ranch into shape.' He had some half-baked idea the two a you was goin a move up here, build a log cabin and help me run this ranch and bring it up. Then, this spring he's got another one's goin a come up here with him and build a place and help run the ranch, some ranch neighbor a his from down in Texas. He's goin a split up with his wife and come back here. So he says. But like most a Jack's ideas it never come to pass."

So now he knew it had been the tire iron. He stood up, said, you bet he'd like to see Jack's room, recalled one of Jack's stories about this old man. Jack was dick-clipped and the old man was not; it bothered the son who had discovered the anatomical disconformity during a hard scene. He had been about three or four, he said, always late getting to the toilet, struggling with buttons, the seat, the height of the thing and often as not left the surroundings sprinkled down. The old man blew up about it and this one time worked into a crazy rage. "Christ, he licked the

stuffin out a me, knocked me down on the bath-
room floor, whipped me with his belt. I thought he
was killin me. Then he says, 'You want a know what
it's like with piss all over the place? I'll learn you,' and
he pulls it out and lets go all over me, soaked me,
then he throws a towel at me and makes me mop up
the floor, take my clothes off and warsh them in the
bathtub, warsh out the towel, I'm bawlin and blub-
berin. But while he was hosin me down I seen he had
some extra material that I was missin. I seen they'd
cut me different like you'd crop a ear or scorch a
brand. No way to get it right with him after that."

The bedroom, at the top of a steep stair that had its
own climbing rhythm, was tiny and hot, afternoon
sun pounding through the west window, hitting the
narrow boy's bed against the wall, an ink-stained
desk and wooden chair, a b.b. gun in a hand-whittled
rack over the bed. The window looked down on the
gravel road stretching south and it occurred to him
that for his growing-up years that was the only road
Jack knew. An ancient magazine photograph of some
dark-haired movie star was taped to the wall beside
the bed, the skin tone gone magenta. He could hear

Jack's mother downstairs running water, filling the kettle and setting it back on the stove, asking the old man a muffled question.

The closet was a shallow cavity with a wooden rod braced across, a faded cretonne curtain on a string closing it off from the rest of the room. In the closet hung two pairs of jeans crease-ironed and folded neatly over wire hangers, on the floor a pair of worn packer boots he thought he remembered. At the north end of the closet a tiny jog in the wall made a slight hiding place and here, stiff with long suspension from a nail, hung a shirt. He lifted it off the nail. Jack's old shirt from Brokeback days. The dried blood on the sleeve was his own blood, a gushing nosebleed on the last afternoon on the mountain when Jack, in their contortionistic grappling and wrestling, had slammed Ennis's nose hard with his knee. He had staunched the blood which was everywhere, all over both of them, with his shirtsleeve, but the staunching hadn't held because Ennis had suddenly swung from the deck and laid the ministering angel out in the wild columbine, wings folded.

The shirt seemed heavy until he saw there was

another shirt inside it, the sleeves carefully worked down inside Jack's sleeves. It was his own plaid shirt, lost, he'd thought, long ago in some damn laundry, his dirty shirt, the pocket ripped, buttons missing, stolen by Jack and hidden here inside Jack's own shirt, the pair like two skins, one inside the other, two in one. He pressed his face into the fabric and breathed in slowly through his mouth and nose, hoping for the faintest smoke and mountain sage and salty sweet stink of Jack but there was no real scent, only the memory of it, the imagined power of Brokeback Mountain of which nothing was left but what he held in his hands.

In the end the stud duck refused to let Jack's ashes go. "Tell you what, we got a family plot and he's goin in it." Jack's mother stood at the table coring apples with a sharp, serrated instrument. "You come again," she said.

Bumping down the washboard road Ennis passed the country cemetery fenced with sagging sheep wire, a tiny fenced square on the welling prairie, a few graves bright with plastic flowers, and didn't want to know Jack was going in there, to be buried on the grieving plain.

A few weeks later on the Saturday he threw all Stoutamire's dirty horse blankets into the back of his pickup and took them down to the Quik Stop Car Wash to turn the high-pressure spray on them. When the wet clean blankets were stowed in the truck bed he stepped into Higgins's gift shop and busied himself with the postcard rack.

"Ennis, what are you lookin for rootin through them postcards?" said Linda Higgins, throwing a sopping brown coffee filter into the garbage can.

"Scene a Brokeback Mountain."

"Over in Fremont County?"

"No, north a here."

"I didn't order none a them. Let me get the order list. They got it I can get you a hunderd. I got a order some more cards anyway."

"One's enough," said Ennis.

When it came—thirty cents—he pinned it up in his trailer, brass-headed tack in each corner. Below it he drove a nail and on the nail he hung the wire hanger and the two old shirts suspended from it. He stepped back and looked at the ensemble through a few stinging tears.

"Jack, I swear—" he said, though Jack had never asked him to swear anything and was himself not the swearing kind.

Around that time Jack began to appear in his dreams, Jack as he had first seen him, curly-headed and smiling and bucktoothed, talking about getting up off his pockets and into the control zone, but the can of beans with the spoon handle jutting out and balanced on the log was there as well, in a cartoon shape and lurid colors that gave the dreams a flavor of comic obscenity. The spoon handle was the kind that could be used as a tire iron. And he would wake sometimes in grief, sometimes with the old sense of

joy and release; the pillow sometimes wet, sometimes the sheets.

There was some open space between what he
knew and what he tried to believe, but nothing could
be done about it, and if you can't fix it you've got to
stand it.

ABOUT THE AUTHOR

Annie Proulx is the acclaimed author of *The Shipping News* and three other novels, *That Old Ace in the Hole,* *Postcards,* and *Accordion Crimes,* and the story collections *Heart Songs, Close Range,* and *Bad Dirt.* Winner of the Pulitzer Prize, a National Book Award, the *Irish Times* International Fiction Prize, two O. Henry Prizes, and a PEN/Faulkner Award, she lives in Wyoming and Newfoundland.